D0835791

This book belongs to....

The
Nursery Collection

Ring-a-Ring o' Roses

This is a Parragon Book
This edition published in 2003

Parragon, Queen Street House, 4 Queen Street, Bath BA1 1HE, UK

Produced by The Templar Company plc

Copyright © Parragon 2000

Edited by Caroline Repchuk
Designed by Kilnwood Graphics

Printed and bound in China
ISBN 1 40540 061 7

The Nursery Collection

Ring-a-Ring o' Roses

Contents

Round and Round
the Garden

Round and round
the garden,
Like a teddy bear.
One step, two steps,
Tickly under there!

Round and round
the haystack,
Went the little mouse.
One step, two steps,
In this little house.

Circle palm

ROUND AND ROUND

Walk fingers up arm

ONE STEP, TWO STEPS

Tickle!

TICKLE!

9

The Wheels on the Bus

The wheels on the bus go round and round,
Round and round, round and round.
The wheels on the bus
go round and round,
All day long.

The wipers on
the bus go swish,
swish, swish, etc.

The horn on the bus
goes beep! beep! beep! etc.

Pat thumb on rest of extended fingers

CHAT, CHAT, CHAT

Pretend to press a horn

BEEP! BEEP! BEEP!

Waggle both extended index fingers

SWISH, SWISH, SWISH

Move fists in a circular motion

ROUND AND ROUND

10

The people on the bus go chat, chat, chat, etc.

The children on the bus bump up and down, etc.

The babies on
the bus go "WAAH!
WAAH! WAAH!", etc.

The grannies on
the bus go knit,
knit, knit, etc.

The wheels on
the bus go round
and round.
All day long.

Bump up and
down on chair

BUMP UP AND DOWN

Make 'uhaa' sound with
hands around mouth

WAAH! WAAH! WAAH!

Pretend to knit with
extended index fingers

KNIT, KNIT, KNIT

Repeat first action

ROUND AND ROUND

11

If You're Happy and You Know It

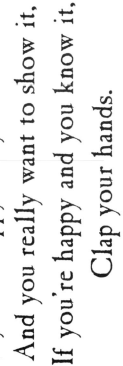

If you're happy and you know it,
Clap your hands.
If you're happy and you know it,
Clap your hands.
If you're happy and you know it,
And you really want to show it,
If you're happy and you know it,
Clap your hands.

If you're happy and you know it,
    Nod your head, etc.
If you're happy and you know it,
    Stamp your feet, etc.

If you're happy and you know it,
    Say "ha, ha!", etc.
If you're happy and you know it,
    Do all four!

13

I Hear Thunder

(To the tune of Frère Jacques)

I hear thunder,
I hear thunder,
Oh! don't you?
Oh! don't you?

Pitter, patter raindrops,
Pitter, patter raindrops,
I'm wet through,
I'm wet through.

Wrap arms around body

I'M WET THROUGH

Flutter hands like rain

PITTER, PATTER RAINDROPS

Pretend to listen

I HEAR THUNDER ...

I see blue skies,
I see blue skies,
Way up high,
Way up high,

Hurry up the sunshine,
Hurry up the sunshine,
I'll soon dry,
I'll soon dry.

WAY UP HIGH

Point up to sky

HURRY UP THE SUNSHINE

Circle hands in front of chest

I'LL SOON DRY

Pretend to shake hands dry

Five Little Peas

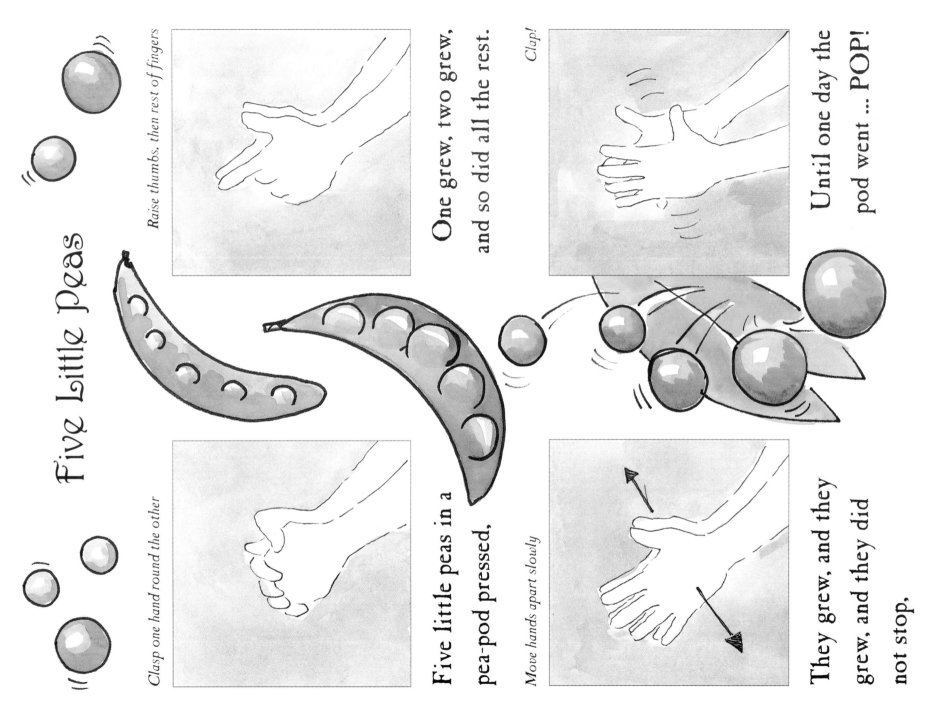

Clasp one hand round the other

Five little peas in a pea-pod pressed.

Raise thumbs, then rest of fingers

One grew, two grew, and so did all the rest.

Move hands apart slowly

They grew, and they grew, and they did not stop.

Clap!

Until one day the pod went ... POP!

One Finger, One Thumb

One finger, one thumb, keep moving,
One finger, one thumb, keep moving,
One finger, one thumb, keep moving,
We'll all be merry and bright.

One finger, one thumb,
one arm, keep moving,
One finger, one thumb,
one arm, keep moving,
One finger, one thumb,
one arm, keep moving,
We'll all be merry and bright.

One finger, one thumb, one arm,
one leg, keep moving, etc

One finger, one thumb,
one arm, one leg, one nod
of the head, keep moving, etc.

This rhyme may be continued with other verses - stand up, sit down, turn around, etc.

17

Five Fat Sausages

Hold up five fingers

FIVE FAT SAUSAGES

Clap!

ONE WENT BANG!

Hold up four fingers

FOUR FAT SAUSAGES

Clap!

...ONE WENT BANG!

Five fat sausages frying in a pan.
All of a sudden one went 'BANG!'
Four fat sausages, etc.
Three fat sausages, etc.
Two fat sausages, etc.
One fat sausage frying in a pan,
All of a sudden it went 'BANG!'
and there were NO sausages left!

ONE FAT SAUSAGE

Continue until one finger left

Clap!

...IT WENT BANG!

NO SAUSAGES!

Two Fat Gentlemen

Two fat gentlemen
met in a lane,
Bowed most politely,
bowed once again.
How do you do?
How do you do?
How do you do again?

Repeat actions for other fingers: two thin ladies = index fingers, etc.

Two thin ladies met in a lane, etc.
Two tall policemen met in a lane, etc.
Two little schoolboys met in a lane, etc.
Two little babies met in a lane, etc.

*Hold out fists
with thumbs raised*

TWO FAT GENTLEMEN ...

Bend each thumb in turn

BOWED MOST POLITELY

*Wiggle each
thumb in turn*

HOW DO YOU DO?

Wiggle thumbs together

HOW DO YOU DO AGAIN?

19

Ten Little Fingers

I have ten little fingers,
And they all belong to me.
I can make them do things.

Would you like to see?
I can shut them up tight,
Or open them all wide.

Hold hands up

TEN LITTLE FINGERS

Waggle fingers

... ALL BELONG TO ME ...

Clench fists

... SHUT THEM TIGHT ...

Open hands wide

... OPEN THEM ALL WIDE

Put them all together,
Or make them all hide.
I can make them jump high;

I can make them jump low.
I can fold them quietly,
And hold them all just so.

Interlock fingers

PUT THEM ALTOGETHER

Place hands behind back

... MAKE THEM ALL HIDE

Move arms up and down

...JUMP HIGH/LOW

Put hands together in lap

HOLD THEM ALL JUST SO

21

This Little Piggy Went To Market

This little piggy went to market,

This little piggy stayed at home,

Wiggle ...

each ...

toe ...

22

This little piggy had roast beef,

This little piggy had none,

And this little piggy cried,

"Wee-wee-wee!"

All the way home.

in ...

turn.

Tickle!

23

The Apple Tree

Here is the tree with leaves so green.
Here are the apples that hang between.
When the wind blows the apples fall.
Here is a basket to gather them all.

Make tree with arms

HERE IS THE TREE

Make fists

HERE ARE THE APPLES

Wave arms then let fists fall suddenly

... THE APPLES FALL

Link hands to make a basket

HERE IS THE BASKET ...

24

The Cherry Tree

Once I found a cherry stone,
I put it in the ground,
And when I came to look at it,
A tiny shoot I found.

The shoot grew up and up each day,
And soon became a tree.
I picked the rosy cherries then,
And ate them for my tea.

Make hole with one hand
and pretend to plant stone

ONCE I FOUND ...

Slowly push finger up
through 'hole'

...A TINY SHOOT I FOUND

Push hand up through
hole, and hold wrist

... SOON BECAME A TREE

Pretend to pick cherry
from each finger and eat!

... ATE THEM FOR MY TEA

Dance, Thumbkin, Dance

Make thumbs dance

Dance, dance, thumbkin, dance.
Dance ye merrymen everyone.
Thumbkin he can dance alone,
He can dance alone.

Dance, dance, foreman, dance.
Dance ye merrymen everyone.
Foreman he can dance alone,
He can dance alone.

26

Dance, dance, longman, dance.
Dance ye merrymen everyone.
Longman he can dance alone,
He can dance alone.

Dance, dance, ringman, dance.
Dance ye merrymen everyone.
Ringman he can dance alone,
He can dance alone.

Dance, dance, babyman, dance.
Dance ye merrymen everyone.
Babyman he can dance alone,
He can dance alone.

Ring A Ring O'Roses

Ring-a-ring o'roses,
A pocket full of posies,
A-tishoo! A-tishoo!
We all fall down!

Dance around in a ring, pretend to sneeze, then fall down on the floor

Pop Goes the Weasel

Half a pound of tu'penny rice,
Half a pound of treacle.
That's the way the money goes,
POP! goes the weasel.

A bouncing on the knee rhyme, with an extra big bounce on the "Pop!"

Here We Go Round the Mulberry Bush

Here we go round the mulberry bush,
mulberry bush, mulberry bush,
Here we go round the mulberry bush,
on a cold and frosty morning.

This is the way we brush our hair,
brush our hair, brush our hair,
This is the way we brush our hair,
on a cold and frosty morning.

Repeat chorus

This is the way we clap our hands,
clap our hands, clap our hands,
This is the way we clap our hands,
on a cold and frosty morning.

Repeat chorus

This is the way we fall on the floor,
fall on the floor, fall on the floor,
This is the way we fall on the floor,
on a cold and frosty morning.

Repeat chorus

Incy Wincy Spider

Incy Wincy spider climbing up the spout,
Down came the rain and washed the spider out.
Out came the sun, and dried up all the rain,
Incy Wincy spider climbed up the spout again.

Wiggle fingers as you lower them

DOWN CAME THE RAIN...

*Touch opposite index fingers and
thumbs together by twisting wrists*

CLIMBING UP THE SPOUT...

*Make a big circle with arms.
Repeat first action.*

OUT CAME THE SUN...

Two Little Men in a Flying Saucer

Two little men in a flying saucer
Flew round the world one day.

They looked to the left and right a bit,
And couldn't bear the sight of it,

And then they flew away.

Move arms up and down

Lift baby in circle

Turn head left

Turn head right

Cover eyes

Repeat first action

34

Tall Shop

Raise arms above head

Tall shop in
the town.

Swing forearms open and shut

Doors swinging round about.

People moving in and out.

Move hands up and down

Lifts moving up
and down.

Move fists back and forth

I'm a Little Teapot

AND STOUT

HANDLE

SPOUT

I'm a little teapot

short and stout,

Here's my handle,

here's my spout,

When I get my

steam up hear me shout,

Tip me up

and pour me out.

SHORT ...

STEAM UP

SHOUT

TIP

POUR

Okey Cokey

You put your left arm in, your left arm out,

In, out, in, out, you shake it all about,

You do the okey cokey, and you turn around,

And that's what it's all about.

Oh, the okey cokey,

Oh, the okey cokey,

Oh, the okey cokey,

Knees bend, arms stretch,

Ra, ra, ra!

Rhyme continues with right arm, left leg,
right leg, whole self.

SHAKE IT ALL ABOUT...

TURN AROUND...

KNEES BEND, ARM STRETCH

LEFT ARM IN...

LEFT ARM OUT...

Build a House with Five Bricks

Place fists on top of each other in turn

Build a house with five bricks,

One, two, three, four, five.

Put a roof on top.

Raise arms for chimney

Make a roof

And a chimney too.

Where the wind blows through!

Blow!

38

Knock at the Door

Knock at the door, (Knock on forehead)

Peep in, (Lift eyebrow)

Lift the latch, (Push nose up)

Ring the bell, (Pull ear)

And walk in. (Put finger in mouth)

39

I Am the Music Man

LEADER: I am a music man,
I come from far away,
And I can play.
What can you play?

ALL: I play piano.
Pia, pia, piano, piano, piano.
Pia, pia, piano, pia, piano.

LEADER: I am a music man,
I come from far away,
And I can play.
What can you play?
I play the big drum.

ALL: Boomdi, boomdi, boomdi boom,
Boomdi boom, boomdi boom, boomdi boom,
Boomdi, boomdi, boomdi, boomdi boom,
Boomdi, boomdi boom.
Pia, pia, piano, piano, piano,
Pia, pia, piano, pia, piano.

LEADER: I am a music man,
I come from far away,
And I can play.

ALL: What can you play?

LEADER: I play the trumpet.

ALL: Tooti, tooti, tooti, toot,
Tooti, toot, tooti, toot,
Tooti, tooti, tooti, toot,
Tooti, tooti, toot.

Boomdi, boomdi, boomdi boom,
Boomdi boom, boomdi boom,
Boomdi, boomdi, boomdi boom,
Boomdi, boomdi boom.

Pia, pia, piano, piano,
Pia, pia, piano, piano,
Pia, pia, piano,
Pia, pia, piano.

Pretend to play each instrument in turn

41

Turn Around

Turn around and touch the ground,
Turn around and touch the ground,
Turn around and touch the ground,
And fall right down.

The Baby in the Cradle

The baby in the cradle
Goes rock-a-rock-a-rock.

The clock on the dresser
Goes tick-a-tick-a-tock.

The rain on the window
Goes tap-a-tap-a-tap.

But here comes the sun,
So we clap-a-clap-a-clap!

Rock arms

ROCK

Swing arm side to side

TICK-TOCK

Tap finger on hand

TAP-A-TAP

Clap!

CLAP

My Hands

My hands upon my head I place,
On my shoulders, on my face;
On my hips I place them so,
Then bend down to touch my toe.

Place hands on head

... on shoulders

... on face

... on hips

Now I raise them up so high,
Make my fingers fairly fly.
Now I clap them, one, two, three.
Then I fold them silently.

Touch toes

Raise hands in the air

Clap hands three times

Fold arms

These Are Grandma's Glasses

These are Grandma's glasses,
  This is Grandma's hat;
Grandma claps her hands like this,
  And rests them in her lap.

Place hands in lap

Clap hands

Mime hat with hands

Make rings round eyes

These are Grandpa's glasses,
  This is Grandpa's hat;
Grandpa folds his arms like this,
  And has a little nap.

Pretend to sleep

Fold arms

Mime hat with hands

Make rings round eyes

46

Mousie

Make a fist and push other index finger in

MOUSIE CREEPING

Push finger through until end appears

MOUSIE PEEPING

Wiggle finger

I'D LIKE TO STAY ...

Pull finger back suddenly and hide!

... POPPED INTO HOLE

Mousie comes a-creeping, creeping, creeping.
Mousie comes a-peeping, peeping, peeping.
Mousie says, "I'd like to stay,
But I haven't time today."
Mousie pops into his hole
And says, "ACHOO!
I've caught a cold!"

47

I Saw a Slippery, Slithery Snake

I saw a slippery, slithery snake
Slide through the grasses,
Making them shake.

Circle eyes

"Go away from my pretty green garden," said I.

He looked at me with his beady eye.

Weave hands side to side

Go away!

"Sssss," said the slippery, slithery snake,
As he slid through the grasses,
Making them shake.

Repeat first action

Foxy's Hole

Put your finger in
Foxy's hole.
Foxy's not at home.
Foxy's out at the
back door
A-picking at a bone.

... FINGER IN FOXY'S HOLE

Interlock fingers leaving a hole
between middle and ring finger

FOXY'S NOT AT HOME

Get child to put finger in hole

A-PICKING AT A BONE

Nip child's finger with thumbs

49

The Beehive

Here is the beehive.
Where are the bees?
Hidden away where nobody sees.
Soon they come
creeping out of the hive,
One, two, three, four, five!

Fold one hand over the other to make hive

BEEHIVE

Slowly bring out thumb ..

THEY COME CREEPING ...

... followed by the other fingers, one by one

... THREE, FOUR ...

Suddenly tickle child!

...FIVE!

With My Hands on Myself

With my hands on myself,
what have we here?
This is my brainbox,
nothing to fear.
Brainbox and wibbly
wobbly woos,
That's what they taught me
when I went to school.

With my hands on myself,
what have we here?
These are my eye-peepers,
nothing to fear.
Eye-peepers, brainbox
and wibbly wobbly woos,
That's what they taught me
when I went to school.

With my hands on myself,
 what have we here?
This is my nose-wiper,
 nothing to fear.
Nose-wiper, eye-peepers,
 brainbox and wibbly
 wobbly woos,
That's what they taught me
 when I went to school.

With my hands on myself,
 what have we here?
This is my chest-protector,
 nothing to fear.
Chest-protector, nose-wiper,
 eye-peepers, brainbox and
 wibbly wobbly woos,
That's what they taught me
 when I went to school.

Wibbly woobly woos are the ear lobes, which should be wiggled whenever they are mentioned. Additional verses could include bread basket (tummy), knee knockers (knees), and shoe stuffers (feet).

Little Cottage in the Wood

Knock fist in air

KNOCKING AT DOOR

Hold up fingers

RABBIT RUNNING

Look through hands

MAN BY THE WINDOW

Make roof with hands

LITTLE COTTAGE

Little cottage in the wood,

Little old man by the window stood,

Saw a rabbit running by,

Knocking at the door.

"Help me! Help me! Help me!" he said,

"Before the huntsman shoots me dead."

"Come little rabbit, come inside,

Safe with me abide."

Stroke hand (rabbit)

SAFE WITH ME

Beckon with same finger

COME INSIDE

Point with one finger

HUNTSMAN SHOOTS

Wave arms up and down

HELP ME!

54

This is the Way the Ladies Ride

This is the way the ladies ride,
Nimble-nim, nimble-nim.

This is the way the gentlemen ride,
Gallop-a-trot, gallop-a-trot.

This is the way the farmers ride,
Hobbledy-hoy, hobbledy-hoy.

This is the way the butcher boy rides,
Tripperty-trot, tripperty-trot.

Till he falls in a ditch with a flipperty,
Flipperty, flop, flop, **FLOP!**

Bounce baby on knee, getting faster as rhyme progresses, and 'dropping' baby through knees on last verse

Jelly on the Plate

Rock from side to side

Blow!

Jelly on the plate,
Jelly on the plate,
Wibble, wobble,
Wibble, wobble,
Jelly on the plate.

Sweeties in the jar,
Sweeties in the jar,
Shake them up,
Shake them up,
Sweeties in the jar.

Candles on the cake,
Candles on the cake,
Blow them out,
Blow them out,
Puff, PUFF, PUFF!

Bounce up and down

Here's the Lady's Knives and Forks

Here's the lady's knives and forks.
Here's the lady's table.
Here's the lady's looking glass.
And here's the baby's cradle.
Rock! Rock! Rock! Rock!

KNIVES AND FORKS...

Interlock fingers with backs of hands together

TABLE...

Turn hands over and bring wrists together

LOOKING GLASS...

Raise both index fingers

CRADLE - ROCK!

Raise both little fingers and rock back and forth

Gee Up, Neddy

Gee up, Neddy,
Don't you stop,
Just let your feet go
Clippety clop.
Clippety clopping,
Round and round.
Giddy up,
We're homeward bound.

Bounce baby on knee

Hickory Dickory Dock

Walk fingers up arm

Hickory
dickory dock,
The mouse ran
up the clock.

Clap once

The clock
struck one,

Walk fingers down arm

The mouse
ran down,
Hickory
dickory dock.

61

Here's a Ball for Baby

Here's a ball for baby,
Big and fat and round.

Here is baby's hammer,
See how it can pound.

Here are baby's soldiers,
Standing in a row.

Here is baby's music,
Clapping, clapping so.

Make ball with hands

BALL

Tap fist against knee

HAMMER

Show ten fingers

SOLDIERS

Clap hands

CLAPPING

62

Here is baby's trumpet,
TOOTLE-TOOTLE-OO!

Here's the way the baby
Plays at peek-a-boo.

Here's a big umbrella,
To keep the baby dry.

Here is baby's cradle,
Rock-a-baby-bye.

TRUMPET — Blow through fist

PEEK-A-BOO — Hands up to eyes

UMBRELLA — Pretend to hold umbrella

CRADLE — Rock hands in cradle

63

As Small as a Mouse

As wide as a bridge.

As straight as a pin.

As small as a mouse,

As tall as a house,

Slowly, Slowly

Slowly, slowly, very slowly
Creeps the garden snail.

Slowly, slowly, very slowly
Up the garden rail.

Quickly, quickly, very quickly
Runs the little mouse.

Quickly, quickly, very quickly
Round about the house.

Walk hand slowly up baby's tummy...

Tickle baby during second verse

Row, Row, Row Your Boat

Row, row, row your boat,
Gently down the stream.
Merrily, merrily, merrily merrily,
Life is but a dream.

Mime rowing action throughout ...

Round About There

Round about there,
Sat a little hare,
A cat came and
chased him,
Right up there!

Circle child's palm with finger

ROUND ABOUT THERE

Walk fingers up arm

A CAT CAME AND CHASED HIM

Tickle!

RIGHT UP THERE!

The Ostrich

Here is the ostrich
straight and tall,

Nodding his head
above us all.

Here is the hedgehog
prickly and small,

Rolling himself
into a ball.

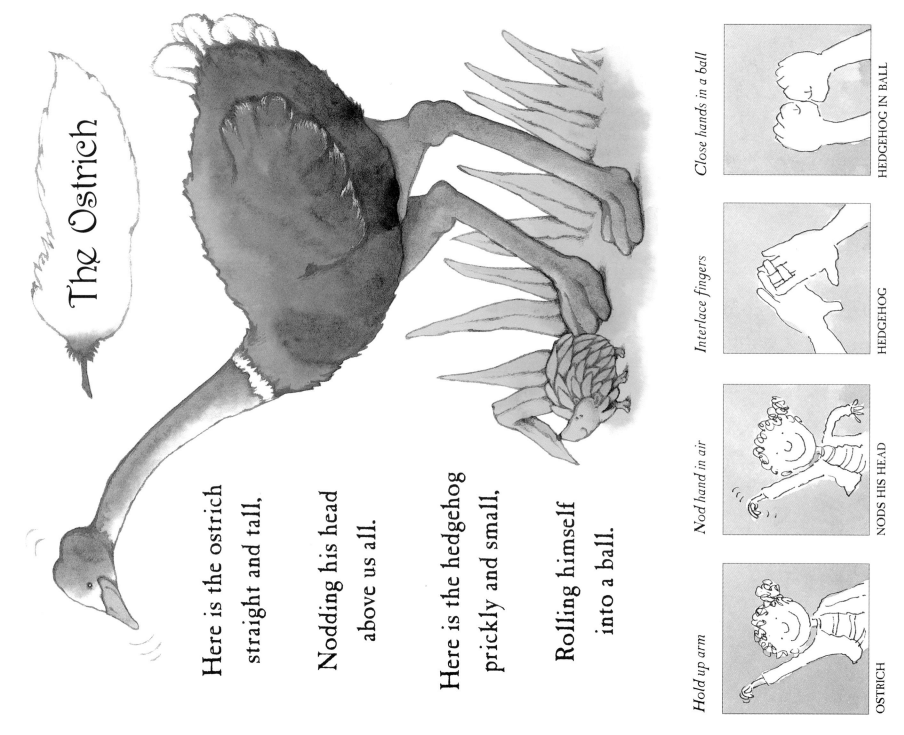

Hold up arm

OSTRICH

Nod hand in air

NODS HIS HEAD

Interlace fingers

HEDGEHOG

Close hands in a ball

HEDGEHOG IN BALL

Here is the spider scuttling around,
Treading so lightly on the ground.
Here are the birds that fly so high,
Spreading their wings across the sky.

Here are the children fast asleep,
And in the night the owls do peep.
"Tuit tuwhoo, tuit tuwhoo!"

SPIDER — *Wriggle fingers*

BIRDS — *Lock thumbs together*

CHILDREN ASLEEP — *Pretend to sleep*

OWLS — *Make rings around eyes*

Five Little Soldiers

Five little soldiers standing in a row,

Three stood straight,

And two stood — so.
Along came the captain,
And what do you think?
They ALL stood straight,
As quick as a wink.

Straighten all fingers

... ALL STOOD STRAIGHT

Pass index finger of other hand in front

... WHAT DO YOU THINK

Fold down two fingers

AND TWO STOOD - SO

Hold five fingers up

FIVE LITTLE SOLDIERS

Here Sits the Lord Mayor

Here sits the Lord Mayor,

Here sit his two men,

Here sits the cocky,

Here sits the hen,

HENHOUSE

Here sit the chicks,

And here they run in,

Chin chopper,
chin chopper,
chin chopper,
     chin.

Clap, Clap Hands

Clap, clap hands, one, two, three,
Put your hands upon your knees,
Lift them up high to touch the sky,
Clap, clap hands and away they fly.

Clap hands in rhythm   *Touch knees*   *Raise arms*   *Shake raised hands*

CLAP, CLAP HANDS   ... YOUR KNEES   ... LIFT THEM HIGH   ... AWAY THEY FLY

Five Little Monkeys

Five little monkeys jumping on the bed,
One fell off and bumped his head,
Mummy phoned the doctor and the doctor said,
"No more monkeys jumping on the bed!"

Four little monkeys...
Three little monkeys...
Two little monkeys...
One little monkey...

FIVE LITTLE MONKEYS

Hold up hand

Repeat actions showing one less finger each time

Pat top of head

... BUMPED HIS HEAD

Pretend to hold phone

... PHONED THE DOCTOR

Waggle index finger

NO MORE MONKEYS ...

There Was a Little Turtle

There was a little turtle,
He lived in a box.
He swam in a puddle,
He climbed on the rocks.

He snapped at a mosquito,
He snapped at a flea.
He snapped at a minnow,
He snapped at me.

Cup both palms, one on top of the other

... LITTLE TURTLE

Draw a square in the air with index fingers

... IN A BOX

Making swimming motion with hand

... SWAM IN A PUDDLE

Waggle all five fingers in crawling motion

... ON THE ROCKS

He caught the mosquito,
He caught the flea.
He caught the minnow,

But... he didn't catch me!

Snap thumb and fingers
together four times

HE SNAPPED ...

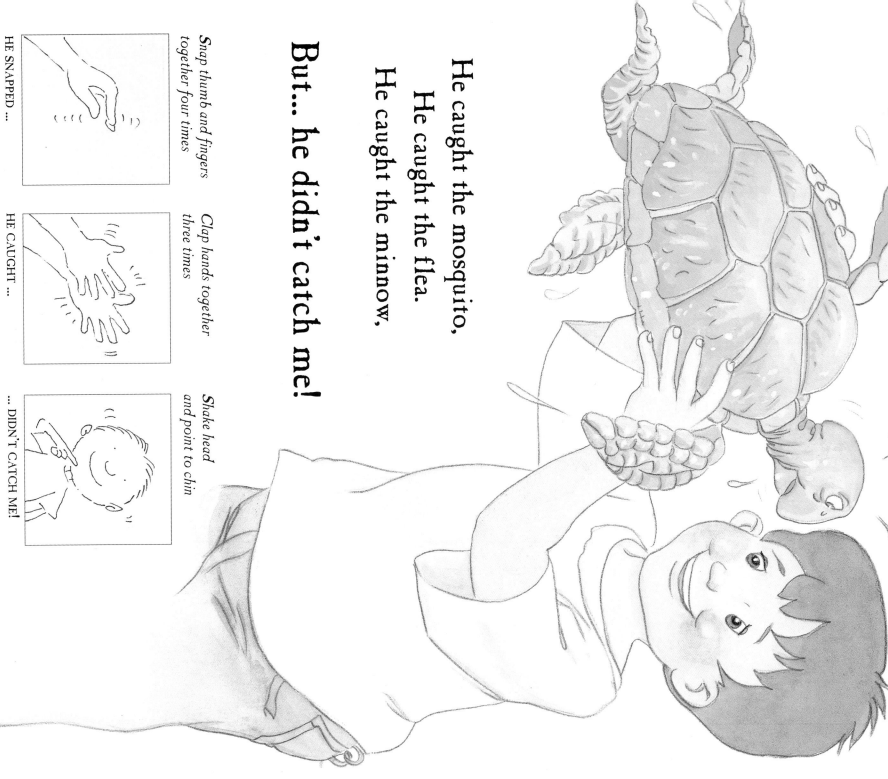

Clap hands together
three times

HE CAUGHT ...

Shake head
and point to chin

... DIDN'T CATCH ME!

75

The Little Bird

This little bird flaps its wings,
Flaps its wings, flaps its wings,
This little bird flaps its wings,
And flies away in the morning!

Link thumbs and flap fingers

THIS LITTLE BIRD ...

Lift hands ...

FLAPS ITS WINGS ...

still flapping ...

FLAPS ITS WINGS ...

as high as you can

FLIES AWAY ...

Two Little Dicky Birds

Stick paper on each index finger

Two little dicky birds
Sitting on a wall,

Toss each hand behind back and bring back middle fingers instead

One named Peter,
One named Paul.

Hold out fingers and shake in turn

Fly away Peter!
Fly away Paul!

Toss each hand behind back and bring back index fingers

Come back Peter,
Come back Paul.

Ten Little Men

Ten little men standing straight,
Ten little men open the gate,
Ten little men all in a ring.

Hold up ten fingers

TEN LITTLE MEN ...

Turn wrists

... OPEN THE GATE ...

Make fingers into ring

... ALL IN A RING ...

Bend fingers

... BOW ...

Dance fingers

... DANCE ...

Hide hands behind back

... HIDE AWAY

Ten little men bow to the king,
Ten little men dance all day,
Ten little men hide away.

79

Scrub Your Dirty Face

Scrub your dirty face,
Scrub your dirty face,
With a rub-a-dub-dub,
And a rub-a-dub-dub,
Scrub your dirty face.

Mime actions. Continue with hands, knees and feet

Clap Your Hands

Clap your hands, clap your hands,
Clap them just like me.
Touch your shoulders, touch your shoulders,
Touch them just like me.
Tap your knees, tap your knees,
Tap them just like me.
Shake your head, shake your head,
Shake it just like me.
Clap your hands, clap your hands,
Then let them quiet be.

I Can ...

I can tie my shoe lace,
I can brush my hair,
I can wash my hands and face
And dry myself with care.

I can clean my teeth too,
And fasten up my frocks.
I can say, "How do you do?",
And pull up both my socks.

Mime actions and put hands in lap at the end

Shoes

Baby's shoes,

Mother's shoes,

Father's shoes,

Policeman's shoes,

GIANT'S SHOES!

Hold hands wider apart for each pair of shoes, and make voice get louder and louder

BABY'S SHOES

MOTHER'S SHOES

FATHER'S SHOES

GIANT'S SHOES!

Dingle Dangle Scarecrow

When all the cows were sleeping
And the sun had gone to bed,
Up jumped the scarecrow
And this is what he said:

I'm a dingle dangle scarecrow
With a flippy floppy hat!
I can shake my arms like this,
I can shake my legs like that!

When the cows were in the meadow
And the pigeons in the loft,
Up jumped the scarecrow
And whispered very soft:
Chorus

When all the hens were roosting
And the moon behind a cloud,
Up jumped the scarecrow
And shouted very loud:
Chorus

84

DINGLE DANGLE

FLIPPY FLOPPY HAT

SHAKE MY ARMS

SHAKE MY LEGS

Peter Works with One Hammer

Peter works with one hammer,
one hammer, one hammer,
Peter works with one hammer,
this fine day.

Peter works with two hammers,
two hammers, two hammers,
Peter works with two hammers,
this fine day.

Peter works with three hammers, etc.
Peter works with four hammers, etc.
Peter works with five hammers, etc.

Bang one fist on knee in rhythm

ONE HAMMER

Bang two fists on knees

TWO HAMMERS

Bang two fists, tap one foot

THREE HAMMERS

Bang two fists, tap two feet

FOUR HAMMERS

Peter's going to sleep now,
sleep now, sleep now,
Peter's going to sleep now,
this fine day.

Peter's very tired now,
tired now, tired now,
Peter's very tired now,
this fine day.

Peter's waking up now,
up now, up now,
Peter's waking up now,
this fine day.

FIVE HAMMERS

Bang two fists, tap two
feet and nod head

TIRED NOW

Rub eyes and stretch
as if yawning

GOING TO SLEEP

Pretend to sleep

WAKING UP

Pretend to wake
and stretch

Pat-A-Cake

Pat-a-cake, pat-a-cake,
baker's man,

Bake me a cake,
as fast as you can.

Pat it and prick it and
mark it with B,

And put it in the oven
for Baby and me.

Put cake in oven

PUT IN THE OVEN

Trace the letter B on palm

MARK IT WITH B

Pat and 'prick' palm

PAT IT, PRICK IT

Clap in rhythm

PAT-A-CAKE

88

Head, Shoulders, Knees and Toes

Head, shoulders, knees
and toes, knees and toes,
Head, shoulders, knees
and toes, knees and toes,

And eyes and ears
and mouth and nose.
Head, shoulders, knees
and toes, knees and toes.

Sing slow at first, then faster.

89

Five Little Ducks

Five little ducks went swimming one day,

Over the hills and far away,

Mother Duck said, "Quack, quack, quack, quack,"

But only four little ducks came back.

Repeat for four, three and two little ducks...

One little duck went swimming one day,

Over the hills and far away,

Mother Duck said, "Quack, quack, quack, quack,"

And all the five little ducks came back.

FOUR LITTLE DUCKS

QUACK, QUACK, QUACK

OVER THE HILLS...

FIVE LITTLE DUCKS...

See-Saw, Margery Daw

See-Saw, Margery Daw,
Johnny shall have a new master,
He shall have but a penny a day,
Because he can't work any faster.

Rock backwards and forwards

92

Here Is the Church

Here is the church,

Interlace fingers

Here is the steeple,

Point index fingers

Open the doors,

And here are
the people

Turn hands over and wiggle fingers

Here is the parson,
going upstairs,

And here he is
a-saying his prayers

*Walk fingers of one hand up
fingers of other hand*

Open thumbs

Place palms together

93

Tommy Thumb

Tommy Thumb,
Tommy Thumb,
Where are you?
Here I am, here I am,
How do you do?

Peter pointer, etc.
Middle Man, etc.
Ruby Ring, etc.
Baby Small, etc.

Raise middle fingers and wiggle them

MIDDLE MAN ...

Raise forefingers and wiggle them

PETER POINTER ...

Make fists, raise thumbs and wiggle them

TOMMY THUMB ...

94

Fingers all, fingers all.
Where are you?
Here we are, here we are,
How do you do?

RUBY RING ...

Raise ring fingers and wiggle them

BABY SMALL ...

Raise little fingers and wiggle them

FINGERS ALL ...

Raise ALL fingers and wiggle them

The End